**TALES OF SHAKESPUSS**

The Three Boxes

Published in Great Britain by
Shakey-Books publishing

Shakey-books
www.shakespuss.com

ISBN 978-0-9955176-0-8

Printed by Lightning Source UK

TALES OF SHAKESPUSS

The Three Boxes

Melissa Mailer-Yates

SHAKEY-BOOKS PUBLISHING

One sunny, winter's day, Shakespuss was lying in his favourite spot by the river.

He was thinking about the story Mr Shakespeare was writing the day before.

He jumped up and reached into his tunic to pull out his magic feather.

In the air he wrote the name of his favourite part of the story in big letters.

He called it 'The Three Boxes'.

As he wrote the words the trees around him became great stone pillars, and he found himself standing in a grand palace.

He called some of his friends to come and pretend to be the people in the story.

This is the story they played.

Once, there was a beautiful girl called Portia.

Her father was very rich and wanted her to marry a prince, but in order to choose the right one he decided they should pass a test.

The test was very odd.

They would be shown three boxes, and they simply had to choose one.

If they chose the box which contained a painting of Portia they could marry her.

However, to make it more difficult, if they chose the wrong box they had to promise never to marry anyone, at all, ever!

The first prince who came to call was the Prince of Morocco.

He was very tall and skinny, and could see no reason why he would choose the wrong box.

With his weedy voice he proclaimed to Portia:

"My dear lady, I am sure you will be very happy with me as your husband. I know I can choose the right box. Now, let me see."

He strutted about with his nose in the air, and went up to the first box which was made of pure gold, and covered with sparkly jewels.

On it was some writing which he read aloud:

"Who chooseth me shall gain what many men desire. Mmm" he pondered, "I know I desire this lovely lady!"

At the second box, which was made entirely of silver, he read the writing:

"Who chooseth me shall get as much as he desires."

His head wobbled a little as he thought, but he sniffed and walked over to the next one.

When he saw the third box he stepped back and held a hanky to his nose as if it smelled.

It was grey, dull, and boring, it didn't shine at all as it was made of lead. However, he still read the words:

"Who chooseth me must give and hazard all he hath."

"Well!" He tossed his head and turned his back on it, "I do not like that!"

"Yeees!" he said to Portia as a wide, sickly smile spread across his face, "Of course, it is the most beautiful one, it has to be the one made of gold ... give me the key!"

He clicked his fingers and rudely snatched it as he was so keen to get the box open.

As he opened the lid with its shiny gold and jewels his face suddenly turned very pale, and his smile vanished.

He lifted a bony skull out that had a little note stuck inside it. When he read the words his legs went all wobbly.

"All that glistens is not gold", the note said. He did not even say goodbye, but just wobbled off on his wobbly legs.

Portia was relieved. "I am rather glad he is not to be my husband! Oh dear, I wonder who will be next?"

In fact the next prince was completely different. He was very short, and bounced nervously around. He was the prince of Aragon.

"Ooh! Hello dear! Ah! Are those the boxes there? Mmm yes, of course they are!"

He hopped over to them and flitted back and forth from one to the other.

"Oh dear, oh dear, gold, silver, an old grey one! I err, this err, oh, I really don't know!"

Finally he stopped at the silver one.

"As much as he deserves?! Ah, well, I do deserve to marry her, it has to be this one."

He flung open the lid and hopped even more when he looked inside. Sure enough, there was a painting.

As he lifted it out everyone held their breath.

When he turned it over he stopped hopping altogether, he didn't see the face of the pretty Portia, instead it was that of a foolish man.

"What's this?!" he cried, "A blinking idiot!"

There was another note too. It explained that he had come with one fool's head, and was leaving with two!

Portia did try to say she was sorry, even though she couldn't help giggle a bit, but before she could say anything the prince bounced out the door and was gone.

"Goodness!" she said, "What a relief, he made me quite dizzy!"

When the next man arrived he was very handsome, his name was Bassanio.

This time Portia did not want him to choose the wrong box, but she was worried he might, so she asked him if he would like to just stay a while instead, perhaps he could choose a box later.

Bassanio was very honourable, "No my gracious lady, I shall do what I came here to do. I must pick a box and trust in my luck."

"Oh, but I am sure you could stay and have some tea or something?" Portia said.

She really didn't want him to go, but he did not want to break the rules, and he needed to get it over with, it was very worrying after all.

To calm him down Portia asked for some music, then if he got it wrong and had to go at least there would be nice music playing.

It may have helped that the words of the song said how important it was to choose with the heart instead of the head.

Certainly Bassanio knew that men can be fooled very easily with things that look pretty and expensive, he also knew that no decoration could ever be as nice as Portia.

So he took his chance and chose the boring, dull, grey box made of lead.

Everyone gasped as he lifted from it the most beautiful painting of her, he had indeed made the right choice.

Both he and Portia were very happy that they would be together forever now.

Everyone cheered and clapped, they all agreed the best man had won for being honest and truthful.

This story is from a play called

'The Merchant of Venice'

written by
William Shakespeare

Shakespuss & Co Ltd

The Players

William Kemp
Festy

Willamena Kemp
Festa

Bottom

Nicholas Tooley
Nick

Josephine Taylor
Jo

Augustine Phillips
Gus

Natalie Field
Nat

Georgina Bryan
Georgie

Samuel Gilburn
Sam

William Shakespuss
Shakey

Lightning Source UK Ltd.
Milton Keynes UK
UKOW07f2353241016
286011UK00010B/107/P

9 780995 517608